DAVID ARO

An imprint of Enslow Publishing

WEST **44** BOOKS™

Meet Me on the Court
Nothing But Net
Swish
Fast Break
Big Shots

Please visit our website, www.west44books.com.
For a free color catalog of all our high-quality books,
call toll free 1-800-542-2595 or fax 1-877-542-2596.

Cataloging-in-Publication Data

Names: Aro, David.
Title: Swish / David Aro.
Description: New York : West 44, 2020. | Series: Alton heights all-stars
Identifiers: ISBN 9781538382158 (pbk.) | ISBN 9781538382165 (library
 bound) | ISBN 9781538383087 (ebook)
Subjects: LCSH: Basketball--Juvenile fiction. | Teamwork (Sports)--
 Juvenile fiction. | Friendship--Juvenile fiction.| Competition (Psychology)--
 Juvenile fiction.
Classification: LCC PZ7.A76 Sw 2020 | DDC [F]--dc23

First Edition

Published in 2020 by
Enslow Publishing LLC
101 West 23rd Street, Suite #240
New York, NY 10011

Editor: Theresa Emminizer
Designer: Seth Hughes

Photo credits: Cover (basketball) undefined undefined/iStock/Thinkstock;
cover (fire) Nixxphotography/iStock/Thinkstock.

Printed in the United States of America

CPSIA compliance information: Batch #CS18W44: For further information contact
Enslow Publishing LLC, New York, New York at 1-800-542-2595.

TYLER
33
CAPTAIN
MARKUS
0
REBOUNDER
JASMINE
11
THE DEFENDER
BRIANNA
2
BALL HANDLER
CAM
23
FLASH FEET

CHAPTER ONE

SUMMER VACATION

It was the All-Stars' most important practice of the year.

Tyler waited by the basketball hoop at the park. He had news to tell his team.

He spun with his hand on the pole. He drew out new plays on the court with a rock. He shot around.

He made five shots in a row from the dotted line. He backed up a step. Made five more. He moved to the free-throw line. Then looked toward the park entrance.

The summer sun shone down on the small trees along the path. The mayor had asked the All-Stars to plant them. Not too long ago, the team had saved the park.

Tyler missed his next two shots. He sat

on the ball. And he waited some more.

The shadows of the trees danced on the ground. And finally, the rest of the All-Stars' shadows joined them.

Tyler ran to his team. "What took you guys so long?"

"Sorry we're late," said Cam.

"Yeah," said Brianna. "Sleeping Beauty over here slept in." She threw grass at Markus.

Markus shook it from his messy hair. "What do you expect? It's the first day of summer vacation."

They walked toward the court. Tyler dribbled the ball.

"I have it all planned out," he said. "We have three weeks. We can meet here every morning. Spend all day practicing for…" Tyler held his breath.

"What is it, already?" asked Markus.

"I-signed-us-up-for-a-tournament-at-the-Rec-Center," said Tyler. As if it was all one word.

"A tournament?" asked Markus. "Do you really think we're ready?"

Brianna stopped laughing. She looked away from Markus. He pulled the last pieces of grass from his hair. Cam started biting his nails. Jasmine stopped walking. She fell behind the rest of the group.

"After all we've been through," said Tyler. "Of course! And now we don't have school or anything else to get in the way of our practice time. It's perfect!"

Tyler passed the ball to Cam. Cam caught it before it hit him in the chest.

"About that," said Jasmine softly. But she was too far back to be heard over Tyler.

"I've made some new plays," said Tyler. "And I think I found someone who can make us team shirts."

"About that," said Jasmine, louder. She walked up to the group.

"I'm sorry," said Tyler. "I couldn't sleep last night. I couldn't wait to tell you guys."

"I don't know how to say this," said Jasmine. Her voice grew quiet.

Tyler paused. Everyone's attention shifted to her.

"What's wrong?" asked Cam.

"I'm not going to be able to practice with you guys," said Jasmine. "I have to live with my dad for the summer."

"Really?" asked Tyler.

Brianna put her arm around Jasmine. "And I thought *I* was the one with bad news," she said.

Jasmine rested her head on Brianna's shoulder. "What's your news?" she asked.

"I have to go to summer school," answered Brianna.

"Me too," said Cam.

Tyler knocked the ball out of Cam's hands. "But neither of you failed any classes!" he said.

"No," said Cam. "But I got a C- in math. So, my mom signed me up. Just to make sure I'm ready for next year."

"And with all our focus on the park," said Brianna. "I never finished the last reading assignment for the year. Now they're making me read extra books. With tests after each one!"

Tyler dropped the ball.

"Speaking of," said Markus.

"You, too?" asked Tyler. He grabbed the sides of his shirt with his fists.

"I have to help my dad mow lawns this summer," answered Markus. "He said I'm old enough to help out. But I'm sure I'll still have time to play. At least a few nights a week."

"It doesn't matter," said Tyler. "There's no point. We can't play in the tournament if we *all* won't be here."

CHAPTER TWO

SOMETHING NEW

Tyler's apartment was spotless. It was his first week of vacation. He had already washed the dishes. Everything smelled like lemon dish soap. He picked up the family room. He took out the trash. He even made his bed. That was something he *never* did.

"What's wrong?" asked Tyler's mom. She opened a drawer. She looked inside. "I'm bored," said Tyler. "And all my friends are too busy to practice."

"Found them." Tyler's mom tossed her car keys into her purse. "I have to get to work," she said. "The house is cleaner than ever. You should get outside. You could always play basketball by yourself."

"Thanks," said Tyler. He rolled his eyes.

Tyler's mom kissed his cheek. She shut the door behind her.

Tyler grabbed the ball. He dribbled around the kitchen. He tossed the ball into the wall. He caught it like it was a pass. He faced the couch. Then shot it. The ball landed in the middle of the couch.

He jumped on the couch after the ball. He laid on his back. He threw the ball in the air. Over and over.

He heard Cam and Brianna's voices as

they came down the hall. They all lived in the Alton Heights housing complex, too.

Tyler threw on his shoes. He ran after them.

"Hey, guys," he called out.

"Hey, Tyler," said Cam.

"What's up?" asked Brianna.

"You guys want to go to the park?" asked Tyler.

Brianna put her book bag over her right shoulder. "Wish we could," she said.

"Yeah," said Cam. "But you're welcome to walk with us."

"It's better than sitting around here," said Tyler.

They reached the park. Cam and Brianna continued on to school. They

disappeared between the houses. Tyler watched from the edge of the court. He was alone, again. Just him, his ball, and…

"Heads up!" shouted T.J. He threw a football from the field towards Tyler.

Tyler turned and caught it.

T.J., Jason, and the rest of the Golden Roots Prep team walked onto the court. Everyone except Steve.

Tyler threw the ball back to T.J. "What are you guys doing here?" he asked. "And where's Steve?"

T.J. threw the ball around his back to Jason. "Steve hurt his ankle at yesterday's practice," he said.

"And the doctor said he has to stay off it for a few weeks," said Jason.

"You guys are still practicing?" asked Tyler. He rolled his shoulders forward.

"Sure are," answered T.J. "I saw your team name on the tournament sign-up list, too. I'm sure you guys have been practicing like crazy."

"Well," Tyler said. "Not exactly. Everyone's so busy. We won't be playing in the tournament."

"Really?" asked T.J. He looked at his teammates. "Well, with Steve out, you can play with us."

Jason nodded in agreement. "Yeah," he said. "We're heading to practice now."

Tyler looked over his shoulder. Cam and Brianna were busy at summer school. The smell of the grass reminded him of Markus working. And Jasmine wasn't even in town.

Tyler picked up his basketball. He couldn't do nothing all summer.

"I'd love to," he said.

CHAPTER THREE

THE OTHER SIDE OF THE FENCE

The Golden Roots Prep gym was different.
Tyler remembered the last time he was there.
Golden Roots fans had booed the All-Stars.

This time, there was no booing. The rest of the All-Stars weren't even there.

Ball racks lined both sides of the court. Blocking dummies were set up for shooting drills on the side hoops.

The Golden Roots Prep coach walked out of the locker room.

"Tyler is going to fill in for Steve," said T.J.

"Welcome aboard," said the coach. "It'll be better playing with you than against you."

"Thanks," said Tyler with a smile.

The coach blew his whistle. "Now, are you guys ready?"

The Golden Roots Prep team clapped.

"Let's do this!" said Jason.

They ran five laps around the gym to warm up. Then the coach put them through some stretches. They stretched their arms. Touched their toes. Then did some skips up and down the court.

The practice was very organized. Way more than Tyler was used to.

They did three-man passing drills

down the court. The players passed the ball to their teammates. Then ran behind them. The last player with the ball made a layup.

"That took six passes," yelled the coach. "Pick it up! You should be able to do that in under five."

Tyler passed the ball to T.J. Then he followed behind him. T.J. passed it to Steve next. Steve passed it back to Tyler. Then Tyler hit T.J. for the layup.

"Four passes," said the coach. "Better. Now, everyone get a ball."

The players all grabbed a ball from the rack. Then they lined up on the baseline in four pairs of two.

In turns, each player dribbled down the court and back with their strong hand. Then they did the same with their weak hand.

Tyler and T.J. were the first pair finished.

"Very good, T.J. and Tyler," said the coach.

T.J. gave Tyler a high five.

"Now, pass the ball between your

legs as you run," said the coach. "*Without* letting it hit the floor."

Both Tyler and T.J. made it back and forth twice without losing the ball. Jason only lost control once. But a few balls rolled around the gym from the other players.

"Is this the kind of effort I expect?" yelled the coach. "Balls up and on the line!"

Everyone put their balls away. Then they lined back up on the baseline.

"When I blow the whistle," said the coach. "Run down and back in under fifteen seconds."

The coach blew his whistle. The kids ran. Up and back. Up and back. Whistle after whistle.

Most of the kids leaned over on their knees between sprints. But Tyler refused to slow down. He ran as fast and hard as he could. There and back. There and back.

He came in first or second every time. He was happy to be practicing with a team.

"Good work, Tyler," said the coach. He

blew the whistle twice. "Get some water."

Practice for the rest of the week went much the same. The week after, too. They did team drills. Ball-handling drills by themselves. Shooting drills. And lots of running in between. Mostly when the team's focus wasn't there.

The only thing that changed from day to day was Tyler. His focus grew sharper. He shot better after the coach used the blocking dummies with him. He was in better shape from all the sprinting in practice. And *also* from the extra running to and from the Golden Roots Prep gym.

"Nice job today, Tyler," said the coach one day after practice. "I wish everyone on the team worked as hard as you do."

"Thanks, Coach," said Tyler.

The rest of the team left. But Tyler wasn't ready to go. He was having too much fun practicing in a fancy gym. In a school that cared about sports.

"Would it be okay if I stayed and shot around a little longer?" he asked.

"No problem," replied the coach.

CHAPTER FOUR

ALONE

Tyler sat on the couch. He watched TV. His mom wasn't home from work yet. And he was beat from the extra work he put in after practice.

There was a knock on the door.

Tyler muted the TV.

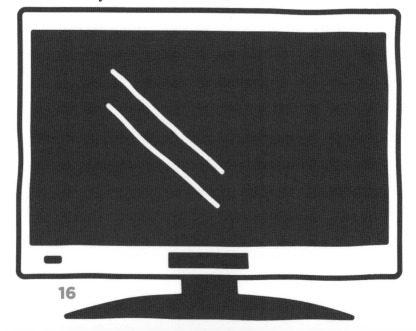

Knock knock.

"Tyler, you home?" asked Markus through the door.

Tyler didn't answer.

"I'm done mowing for the day," said Markus. "I thought we could hang out."

Tyler stayed still. Until after he heard Markus's footsteps on the stairs. And until Markus closed the door to his apartment.

Tyler turned off the TV. He went to bed. He had never ignored one of his friends before. He kept telling himself he was just too tired.

But the next morning, Tyler paused when he put his hand on the doorknob. He could hear Cam and Brianna in the hall. They were leaving for summer school. He waited until the front door closed. Then Tyler ran to the family room window.

He watched them cross the parking lot. They walked down the sidewalk together, laughing.

Tyler didn't realize how much he had missed his friends. And how guilty he felt playing on another team. Especially Golden

Roots Prep.

But he didn't have a choice.

It was the only way he could play basketball. It was how he could play in the Rec Center tournament.

So, Tyler kept sneaking in and out of the Alton Heights housing complex. He left after he knew his friends were gone. And he shut the door to his apartment as quietly as he could when he returned.

But a week and a half out from the tournament, everything changed.

Tyler showed up to practice. He beat the rest of the team, as usual. The coach got out the balls. Tyler shot around. Then T.J., Jason, and the rest of the Golden Roots Prep team came into the gym. Even Steve.

Steve didn't have crutches. Or walk with a limp. He carried a gold and blue gym bag on his shoulder.

Tyler tried his best to keep shooting. But he saw Steve walk over to the coach.

T.J., Jason, and the rest of the guys picked up balls and started shooting around with Tyler.

"Good morning, guys," said Tyler.

"'Sup," said T.J.

"Do you *ever* take a break?" asked Jason.

Before Tyler took another shot, the coach yelled for him. "Tyler. Would you come here a minute?"

Tyler ran over to the side of the court. "Yeah, Coach?"

"Have a seat, will you?" said the coach.

The coach sat with Tyler on the bench.

"It's been a pleasure having you on the team," he said. "I hate to do this to you. But there is a maximum of eight players per team for the tournament. Steve is healthy again. I have no choice but to let him play."

Tyler watched Steve lace up his sneakers. He took his place back on the court. With *his* team. They got ready for warm-ups.

Tyler turned back to the coach. "I understand," he said. He shook the coach's hand. "Thanks for everything."

Tyler walked out of the gym. The wind slammed the door behind him.

Tyler hadn't thought about this. How things might come to an end. He didn't really belong. Even if he won the tournament for Golden Roots Prep. It wouldn't change anything.

When school started, he wouldn't go there. So, he couldn't *really* be a part of their team.

Tyler took his time walking home. He stopped by the park. He sat on the benches. He stared into space. He did his best to block out the playground laughter.

When it got dark, Tyler found his way home. He crawled into his bed. Then held the blankets over his head.

CHAPTER FIVE

A DREAM

Tyler fell asleep before his mom got home. And he stayed in bed the next morning.

"You sure you're okay?" asked his mom through the door. She was about to leave for work.

Tyler grunted. Like she was waking him up. But Tyler wasn't *really* asleep. He had watched his clock tick away most of the night. He had counted the specks in the ceiling. He imagined they were little stars

21

in the sky. He wished on them. Then rolled over onto his side.

He fell in and out of sleep. He couldn't wait for summer to be over. Then things could go back to normal.

Tyler dreamed of playing basketball with his friends. He woke to the sound of a ball bouncing. Then he heard what sounded like Cam, Markus, and Brianna outside.

Tyler jumped out of bed. He put on his shoes and ran outside.

It wasn't a dream! Cam, Markus, and Brianna were taking turns shooting a ball against the building.

"He's alive!" said Cam.

"I've stopped by your house every night for the past week," said Markus. "Where have you been?"

Brianna tossed the ball to Tyler. Tyler held the ball tightly in his hands. He looked at the brick wall they used as a backboard. Then passed the ball back to Brianna.

"I have something to tell you," said Tyler.

The four of them sat on a patch of grass. Tyler told them everything. How he felt alone. How he practiced with Golden Roots Prep. And how Steve had come back. Which made Tyler miss the All-Stars even more.

"With *them*?" asked Brianna. Her lips curled.

Tyler lowered his head.

Cam put his hand on Tyler's shoulder. "To be honest," he said. "I felt like the one that let *you* down."

Brianna stopped making a face. "Cam's right," she said.

"Did you just admit you were wrong?" asked Markus.

Brianna chucked the ball at Markus. Then she looked back at Tyler. "But we have some news that might cheer you up," she said.

"We've both worked so hard in summer school," said Cam. "We're done!"

Tyler rubbed his eyes. He couldn't tell if he was still in bed dreaming.

"And my dad told me he wanted me

to have fun with the rest of my summer," said Markus. "I only have to help out two mornings a week."

Cam stood up. He kicked the ball in the air with his foot. He caught it. "So, do you guys want to go to the park?"

"Sure do," answered Markus.

"You know it," answered Brianna.

Cam helped Tyler off the ground.

"Definitely," said Tyler.

Tyler showed his friends new drills. The ones he had learned from Golden Roots Prep.

First, Tyler warmed them up. Then he showed them how to work on their ball handling. They dribbled the ball as close to the ground as they could. Around their left legs. Then their right legs. Then in a figure eight between both legs.

"This is great!" said Brianna. These drills were easy for her. She was already a great ball handler.

Markus's running had gotten better. Thanks to all the mowing.

"Not bad," said Tyler, after the fifth sprint. Markus didn't even need to rest.

"Don't tell me you guys are having all the fun without me," said Jasmine. She walked toward the basketball court.

Brianna ran to her. She gave her a big hug. "What are you doing back so soon?"

"My dad got a new job," she said. "He has to do some traveling."

"Does that mean you're back?" asked Cam.

"Sure does," answered Jasmine. "I hope I didn't miss too much?"

Tyler stared down the path he had taken to Golden Roots Prep. Then he looked back to his friends. *His* team.

"Actually," he said, "there are still a few days before the tournament. And we *are* already signed up."

"Sounds good to me," said Jasmine. "Where do we start?"

CHAPTER SIX

BACK TOGETHER

The All-Stars got to work.

They walked through their play—Up.

"Good job, guys," said Cam.

Tyler also showed them some of his new plays. Down. Open. And Jam.

"You must have spent a lot of time thinking of these," joked Brianna. "Maybe you do belong in a school with a *real* sports program."

"I'm fine right here," said Tyler. He tossed the ball to Brianna at the top of the key. "Let's run it again."

They ran each play over and over. They made sure they got it just right. Brianna hit Jasmine with a perfect pass as she came off a screen. She knocked down the shot.

It was like they had been practicing together all summer.

Tyler even walked them through some of the Golden Roots plays. "This way, we'll know how to defend them better," he said.

"Do we have game film to go over like a pro team, too?" asked Markus.

They all laughed.

The All-Stars did extra workouts to and from the park. One day, they skipped the whole way there. Then they did defensive slides the whole way back.

"What the heck are you doing?" yelled someone from a car window.

But the All-Stars didn't stop. They wanted to be ready.

Some mornings, Markus had to work with his father. They all chipped in. Jasmine and Brianna raked leaves. Tyler, Cam, and Markus pushed wheelbarrows filled with mulch. Markus's father paid them two dollars each.

That reminded Tyler of their team shirts. "Maybe we could pool our money together. We could get the shirts I told you about?" he said.

"That's a great idea!" said Jasmine.

"Do you think it will be enough?" asked Cam.

The All-Stars counted their money.

"Not quite," said Markus.

"We're almost halfway there," said Tyler.

They spent the last weekend before the tournament collecting soda cans. They picked up loose cans from the park. They swung by Lil Scoops. The owner gave them a plastic bag full. Then they knocked on each door of the Alton Heights housing complex. Even the owner's.

"You guys are looking to make a little extra money, are you?" asked the owner.

"We're trying to raise money for team shirts," explained Tyler.

"I'll tell you what," said the owner. "Scrub the graffiti off the side of building 110. I'll give you the rest of what you need."

"Deal!" said Cam.

The owner handed the All-Stars buckets, brushes, and soap. Then he showed the kids where to fill the buckets with water.

The All-Stars worked the rest of the day. The next day, too. They made sure to get every last speck off the building. And Monday morning, they placed the order for their team shirts.

"Any chance they'll be done in time for our tournament?" asked Tyler.

"I'll put a rush on them," said the T-shirt guy. "They will be done by Thursday."

The team shirts were ready just in time. And they came out better than the All-Stars expected. They were brick-red shirts with white writing. "Alton Heights" was written above a basketball hoop. "All-Stars" was written below.

"I think we're as ready as we're going to be," said Cam. He tried on his team shirt over his other shirt.

"I just hope it's enough," replied Brianna.

"As long as we're all together, and we give it our best," said Tyler. "That's all that matters."

CHAPTER SEVEN

TOURNAMENT RULES

The Rec Center hallway was painted with handprints in every color of the rainbow. Some were arranged in the shapes of grass, flowers, and the sun. There were two big trees. And a bunch of butterflies filled the space above.

The All-Stars could hear the sound of sneakers squeaking from the

gym. They made their way through the crowd.

"Excuse me," said Tyler. He stepped between two adults to get to the sign-in table.

Jasmine pointed to the tournament board on the wall. "Look," she said. "We're playing the 3-Point Bombers first."

All-Stars

vs.

3-Point Bombers

"Golden Roots Prep already won their first game," said Markus.

"We have to win two games in a row to see them in the championship," said Cam. He tucked in his new team shirt.

"One game at a time," said Tyler.

"Are you guys the Alton Heights All-Stars?" asked the man at the sign-in table.

"That's us," said Brianna.

The man got up from the table. He walked over to the gym doors. He held both his hands to his mouth and yelled. "The Alton Heights All-Stars are here." He looked back at the All-Stars. "You guys better hurry. Your game is about to start!"

"But our game doesn't start until ten," said Tyler.

"The first game was a forfeit. One of the teams didn't show," said the man. "The Rim Rockers got a bye into the semifinals. We moved your game up."

"But that's not fair!" said Brianna.

The buzzer went off in the gym.

"Do you want to argue? Or do you want to play?" asked the man.

"Come on, guys," said Tyler. He pulled Brianna's arm.

The All-Stars set their bags down on

their bench.

The 3-Point Bombers were already standing at center court. So were two men in gray Rec Center shirts with whistles.

"We don't even get to warm up?" asked Markus.

"Sorry," said one of the refs. "We need to keep the games moving."

Tyler won the jump. But Brianna threw the ball behind Cam on the wing. It bounced out of bounds.

"My bad," said Brianna.

The All-Stars ran back on defense.

One of the 3-Point Bombers looked to shoot from the elbow. Cam jumped in the air to block the shot. The Bomber rushed to get the shot off. Markus grabbed the rebound.

Brianna called out one of their new plays. "Open!"

The All-Stars spread out wide on the court. Brianna beat her defender off the dribble. She took it all the way to the hoop herself.

The All-Stars were the first team on the board. Then Jasmine stole the inbounds pass. She scored a quick layup. But the ref blew the whistle.

"No basket," he said.

"What are you talking about?" asked Brianna.

"There's no defense in the backcourt," said the ref.

"Since when?" asked Cam.

"Tournament rules," said the ref. He handed the ball back to the 3-Point Bombers.

It took a few trips up and down the court. But the All-Stars got into their groove. Jasmine stole a pass. She hit Cam for a fast-break basket. Markus grabbed three more rebounds.

Brianna dribbled by her defender again. This time, she passed it to Tyler for a jump shot.

In the second half, the All-Stars didn't run one of their set plays. They were clearly better than the 3-Point Bombers. The Bombers tried to shoot as many shots from behind the arc as they could. But most of their shots hit the front of the rim. Or they hit hard off the back rim. The long rebounds gave the All-Stars plenty of fast-break points.

The All-Stars won! And their team moved to the next round on the board.

"Are there any *other* tournament rules we should know about?" asked Cam.

The man turned from the board. "What are you so worried about?" he asked. "You guys still won."

CHAPTER EIGHT

SMOOTH SAILING

The second round wasn't so easy.

The Ankle Breakers were better than the 3-Point Bombers. They were quicker. And they liked to drive to the basket instead of taking shots from the outside. Luckily, the All-Stars played good team defense.

The Ankle Breakers' point guard crossed over the ball. He dribbled past Brianna. Jasmine stepped in. She forced him to make a wild pass out of bounds.

Markus had four blocked shots by the end of the game. Cam had three steals. The player Jasmine guarded only dribbled by her once. Tyler had stepped in. He drew an offensive foul.

The All-Stars won again!

Markus's father brought over orange slices and water. "After two games in one day, you need to drink up and eat," he said.

"Thanks," said Jasmine.

"Yeah, thanks, Dad," said Markus. "The oranges always helped when we were working out in the sun all day."

"It looks like you're going to have your work cut out for you tomorrow," said Markus's father.

Markus tossed an orange peel back into the bag. Brianna wiped the juice dripping down her chin. Tyler set down his water. Cam and Jasmine stared at the court.

The All-Stars were going to play in the championship game against the winner of the game that was happening now. Golden Roots Prep was facing the Rim Rockers. And Golden Roots Prep was losing.

"Look at those guys!" said Markus.

The Rim Rockers looked like they were one or two years older. Their two big men, Curtis and Mo, were six feet tall. Their shoulders were almost taller than T.J. and Steve.

Curtis got the ball on the block. He drop-stepped toward the hoop like it was a drill, and Steve wasn't even there.

"Let's go, Golden Roots!" yelled Tyler from

73"

Curtis & Mo

71"

70"

the stands.

"Keep it together!" yelled Brianna.

But that was easier said than done.

The Rim Rockers' guards were super fast. *And* they had fresh legs. They pressured Jason at the top of the key. It made it hard for him to set up plays. When Golden Roots Prep did move the ball, Curtis and Mo kept blocking shots.

Play after play, the Rim Rockers grew their lead by pounding the ball down low. Then they stole the ball. Mo dunked it on the fast break. And the game was out of reach for Golden Roots Prep.

"How are we going to stop them?" asked Cam.

"I have no idea," answered Tyler.

CHAPTER NINE

HEAD IN THE GAME

The All-Stars got to the Rec Center early the next morning.

Tyler grabbed a ball off the rack. "Come on, guys," he said. "We don't have time to waste."

The All-Stars walked through each of their plays. Twice. They stopped when the Rim Rockers arrived.

Curtis and Mo slapped the wall above the gym door.

"They look even bigger than they did from the stands," said Markus.

The All-Stars did their layups. Jasmine defended Brianna from sideline to sideline. Brianna practiced her ball handling. Cam jumped up and down. He wanted to make sure he was loose. Markus practiced his bank shots.

T.J. walked up to the bleachers. "Good luck, Tyler," he said. He sat behind the All-Stars' bench with Jason and Steve.

Tyler still felt hurt for how things had ended between him and the Golden Roots Prep team. He tried to ignore them. He took deep breaths and shot free throws. Then the buzzer went off.

The All-Stars were as ready as they were going to be.

Tyler stood next to Mo at center court. Mo was at least six inches taller.

Mo won the tip. The All-Stars hurried back on defense.

Curtis posted up Markus on the block. Markus tried to keep Curtis from getting closer to the basket. He held his arm on Curtis's back. Curtis bounced the ball as he leaned into Markus.

The ref blew his whistle. "Foul!"

Markus held his hands in the air.

"You can't push with your arm like that," said the ref.

"What else am I supposed to do?" asked Markus. "He's pushing me!"

"You have to move your feet," answered the ref.

On the inbound, Curtis tipped in the pass for an easy two.

Brianna brought the ball up the court. Her defender met her right at half court. She held her left hand out to guard the ball in her right.

"Down," she called out.

Jasmine moved from the left wing to the left block. She tried to set a pick on Curtis. But he pushed right through her shoulder. He turned her sideways. Markus couldn't get open.

On the other side, Tyler did something he had learned when he practiced with Golden Roots Prep. He set up Mo by taking a step away from Cam's screen. He then rubbed shoulder to shoulder with Cam. Mo couldn't fit between them. Tyler gained a step on Mo. He caught Brianna's pass on the wing.

Tyler looked to pass it. But it was hard to see through Mo's big arms. They moved in whatever direction Tyler held the ball. Tyler gave a pump fake in the air like he was going to shoot. Mo jumped high in the air to block it. Tyler dribbled around him toward the hoop.

He went to shoot a layup on the right side. Curtis came over to help out. He reached across Tyler to block it. Mo tried to block it from behind, too. Curtis and Mo knocked Tyler out of the air onto the ground.

"Foul!" called out the ref.

"Good move," yelled Jason from the stands.

Cam and Jasmine helped Tyler off the ground. He missed both free throws.

"Don't worry about it!" screamed T.J.

The All-Stars did everything they could

think of to keep the ball away from Curtis and Mo. Cam, Jasmine, and Brianna played tight defense on their men. They tried to stop the guards from passing the ball inside.

The added pressure helped. Jasmine tipped the ball as it was being passed. Then she picked up the loose ball. Cam picked off the point guard's pass to the wing. But they couldn't stop the ball from getting inside every time. Tyler and Markus had a hard time stopping Curtis and Mo from scoring. They were just too big.

"I don't know what else we can do," said Markus at halftime. He drank some water.

"We have to tire *them* out on defense," said Jasmine. She tried to catch her breath.

The All-Stars started the second half by taking their time. They ran their plays over and over. Up. Down. Spread. They passed the ball back and forth. They waited for one of the Rim Rockers to fall out of position. And a shot to open up.

Jasmine nailed a shot from the wing.

Markus made a bank shot from outside the paint. Cam beat his man off the dribble. He floated the ball over Curtis's reach. But Tyler couldn't seem to get a shot off when he made a move inside. Curtis or Mo kept fouling him.

"I'm sorry, guys," said Tyler during a time-out. "I'm blowing it. I can't get a clean shot."

"What are you talking about?" asked Cam. "Curtis and Mo are in foul trouble because of you. And we're only down eight!"

"Yeah," said Brianna. "Keep your head in the game."

CHAPTER TEN

LUCKY

The All-Stars' plan started to work. Tyler kept attacking inside. And Mo was taken out of the game with four fouls. One more and he would foul out.

On the All-Stars' next play, Brianna drove baseline. Curtis stepped over to stop her. Brianna found Markus in front of the hoop. Curtis jumped back to block the ball and slapped Markus's arms. Curtis picked up his third foul.

Markus made the first of his two free throws. The second bounced off the side of the rim. Curtis reached over Tyler to get the rebound.

"Foul!" yelled the ref.

Curtis got in the ref's face. "You've got to be kidding me. I barely touched him."

The ref blew his whistle again. "Technical foul!"

Curtis fouled out of the game.

"Boo!" screamed the Rim Rockers from the bench.

Curtis pulled his jersey from his shorts. Then he sat on the bench.

Tyler made both free throws from the technical. The All-Stars were now within six points.

The All-Stars quickly took charge without Curtis and Mo in the game. Tyler came off a screen. He had his first open look of the game. Markus picked up his first block. Cam stole a pass and had a fast-break basket.

There were two minutes left to play.

The score was tied. And Mo subbed back into the game. He scored right away.

The All-Stars called their last time-out.

"If we're going to stop him," said Tyler, "we're going to have to do it together."

Out of the time-out, the All-Stars scored off their play, Up. Then they talked defense.

"Switch," called out Tyler to Markus, after he got caught up in a screen.

Mo beat Markus off the dribble. Tyler fought through the screen in time to help out. But he fouled Mo reaching for the ball.

Mo missed the first free throw. He made the second.

"Jam," called out Brianna.

She passed the ball to Cam on the wing. Markus moved from one block. He set a pick on Mo on the other. Tyler came off the screen and caught the pass in the short corner. His back was to the basket. He faked to his right. Then he spun baseline. He reached his right arm out and shot a reverse layup. The rim kept Mo from blocking the shot.

The All-Stars were back up one.

The Rim Rockers had the ball. Twenty seconds left to play.

Mo posted up on the block. Markus guarded in front of Mo. Tyler stood behind him. The Rim Rockers passed the ball around the three-point line. Mo followed the ball. He got position on the other block.

Mo caught the ball. Tyler stood his ground with his arms in the air. Mo backed into Tyler. They bumped into one another. Mo turned into the lane. But Markus was there waiting for him. Before Mo could turn back the other way, Jasmine snuck in from behind and stole the ball.

She quickly passed it out to Brianna. Brianna passed it ahead to Cam. He dribbled in a big circle on the other side of the court. One of the Rim Rocker guards chased him. The final buzzer went off. Cam threw the ball up into the air.

"We did it!" yelled Markus.

The All-Stars jumped in the air. They gave each other one giant high five. Then they lined up to shake the Rim Rockers' hands.

"Good game," said Tyler.

"You were lucky," said Curtis.

Afterwards, Markus laid down on the court in front of their bench. Cam loosened the laces on his shoes. Jasmine took a sip of water. Brianna wiped her face with a towel.

Tyler watched T.J., Jason, and Steve walk out of the gym with the crowd.

"What is it?" asked Brianna. She threw the towel at Tyler.

Tyler looked back to *his* team. "Curtis was right about one thing," he said. "We are lucky. Lucky to have each other."

Want to Keep Reading?

Turn the page for a sneak peek
at the next book in the series.

9781538382172

CHAPTER ONE

THE LETTER

Tyler ran up and down the hall. He knocked on Cam's door. Markus's door. Then on Jasmine's door. Brianna and Jasmine both answered. Brianna had slept over Jasmine's.

"Let's go," he said. "We got mail!"

The All-Stars didn't know what Tyler was so excited about.

"Don't you know what time it is?" asked Markus at first. Then he saw Cam jump down three steps. Brianna used the handrail. She swung over four steps at once. And Jasmine ran down the stairs without shoes. Markus slammed his door. He followed the other All-Stars to Tyler's apartment.

"So why did you wake us up so early?" asked Markus.

"Early?" asked Brianna. "It's almost noon!" She threw a couch pillow at Markus. It hit his head. "There. I fixed your hair for you." She laughed.

Markus ran his hand through his hair as he sat. Then he yawned.

Tyler held a letter out.

"This came in the mail today," he said. "It's from the Rec Center. It's addressed to the Alton Heights All-Stars! I couldn't open it without you guys."

"What are you waiting for?" asked Cam.

The All-Stars huddled around Tyler. He ripped the envelope open and read.

Dear Alton Heights All-Stars,

Congratulations on winning the Rec Center Tournament! It is our honor to present you with a free entry into the citywide youth basketball tournament on Labor Day weekend. Please use your award code when you sign up online. Best of luck!

"I can't believe it!" said Jasmine.

"I never thought *we* could actually play in a tournament that big," said Cam. He jumped up and down. "It's at Crimson University!"

"I'm sure Golden Roots Prep is in, too," said Brianna.

Markus rubbed his eyes. He stared at the letter again. Then looked to his team. "We barely beat the Rim Rockers at the last tournament. Do you think they'll be there, too?"

Tyler set the letter down on the coffee table.

"I don't know," he said. "But only the best of the best will be there. And that includes us!"

ABOUT THE AUTHOR

David Aro is a former Collegiate All-American basketball player and conference player of the year. In college, he scored over 1,900 points, broke his school's record for the most three-pointers ever made, and also finished in the top 10 in rebounds, steals, and assists. While coaching college basketball, he earned a master's degree in executive leadership and change. Today, he coaches his kids and follows his passion of writing children's books. You can visit him online at www.davidaro.com.

Check out more books at:

www.west44books.com